In the year 874, Vikings ruled the waves, sailing the seas in their powerful Longships. And in a small village called Snekkevik, Freya, Wulf and Vik were born. On the same day!

When Vik lost his parents in a great battle a year later, he was adopted by Freya and Wulf's family, who took him in as their own son.

But Vik and Wulf never did see eye to eye...

"I'M THE LEADER!"

FOR
ELLIE & GUNNAR

First published in 2008 by Orchard Books
First paperback publication in 2009

ORCHARD BOOKS
338 Euston Road, London NW1 3BH
Orchard Books Australia
Level 17/207 Kent St, Sydney, NSW 2000

ISBN 978 1 84616 716 4 (hardback)
ISBN 978 1 84616 724 9 (paperback)

Text and illustrations © Shoo Rayner 2008

1 3 5 7 9 10 8 6 4 2 (hardback)
1 3 5 7 9 10 8 6 4 2 (paperback)

Printed in Great Britain

Orchard Books is a division of Hachette Children's Books,
an Hachette Livre UK company.

www.hachettelivre.co.uk

AND THE TROLLS

SHOO RAYNER

ORCHARD BOOKS

"I hate picking cloudberries. It gives me backache," Vik moaned.

"Me too," Wulf grumbled.

Freya sighed. "Remember what Dad said before he sailed away – if you really help Mum this summer, he'll take one of you on a raiding trip next year."

"That's the only reason I'll pick
the stupid berries," said Vik.

"That's why I've got an extra large
backpack," Wulf smirked. "The more
I pick, the more Mum will tell Dad to
choose me!"

Freya frowned. "It's so unfair. Why can't girls go on the Longships?"

Wulf grabbed Freya's pigtails and pushed his face in hers. "Because you're weak and pathetic, little sister!"

Freya squealed. "Just because you're ten minutes older than me, it doesn't make you the boss!"

Moments later, Vik and Wulf were brawling on the rocky ground. Flek barked and nipped their heels. Freya scrambled to get out from beneath the mayhem.

It was a normal day in Snekkevik.

LONGSHIPS

The Vikings like to spend their summer holidays raiding and robbing and fighting!

Longships can sail across the sea and up small rivers to attack unsuspecting villages.

"Deliver us from the fury of the Northmen, oh Lord." *Anglo-Saxon prayer*

Mum stormed across the yard. "What is going on? Do you want me to tell your father that you spent the whole summer fighting? He told you to be helpful!"

Vik and
Wulf hung
their heads
and stared at
their boots.

"You should be up in those hills by now. Off with you! And don't come back until you've picked every single cloudberry."

Flek bounced ahead, leading the little gang up to the mountains.

"And don't go over the Troll Bridge!" Mum called after them. "Stay on this side of the river. I don't want you fighting with those horrible boys who live over there."

Just beyond the stinky
midden, where the village
dumped all its rubbish,
the path split in two.

"This way,"
Wulf announced.

"But that's the way
to the Troll Bridge,"
said Vik.

"That's where the sun shines longest," Wulf explained. "The berries are bigger and sweeter over there."

"But what about the Trolls?" Vik asked nervously.

"You're not scared of Trolls, are you?" Wulf was much bigger and stronger than Vik. Vik tried to stare him out but he was beaten by Wulf's cruel, ice-blue eyes.

Wulf smirked and
stomped off towards
the Troll Bridge.

"We'd better go with him," Vik told
Freya. "Sticking together is one rule
we must never break."

RULES OF THE VIKINGS

1. **Stick together.**

2. **Fight hard.**

3. **Play hard.**

4. **Be strong.**

5. **Keep fit.**

6. **Go raiding at least once a year on the Longships.**

7. **Don't get seasick.**

8. **Keep your weapons sharp.**

9. **Spend the summer getting ready for the winter.**

10. **Eat everything, even if it's disgusting.**

The Troll Bridge crossed a deep, dark gorge. Halfway over, Flek stopped and growled. The fur stood up on the back of his neck.

"What's the matter, Flek?" Vik hissed. "What's wrong?"

A low, hollow voice boomed from under the bridge. "WHO – GOES – THERE?"

Wulf laughed.
"There's no such
thing as Trolls!"

"Well, I'm not
waiting to find out."
Vik turned back.
"Let's go!"

But Wulf ran over
the bridge. "Come
on! This way!"

Freya looked scared. Vik
grabbed her hand and
dragged her over the bridge.
"We can't let the idiot go
on his own," he explained.

Hideous laughter rolled around
the ravine behind them.

"I hope we don't have to come
back this way!" wailed Freya.

24

TROLLS

Trolls are found all across Scandanavia.

They live in dark places underground.

Trolls are big and hairy and mean and angry and very, very dangerous!

"Wulf was right," said Vik. "The berries are much bigger up here."

"Mmmmmm!" Freya agreed. "And they are so-o-o-o sweet!"

Wulf was hard at work, picking the juicy yellow fruits. "If you stopped eating them, you'd fill your baskets much more quickly," he told them.

Vik stood up and stretched his aching body. "My back hurts. I think we should head home now."

"Just a few more," said Wulf.

a sighed. Her twin brother
win at everything, even
berry-picking!

"You are
so sad," she
told him.

Wulf stuck
his tongue
out. "You're
just a loser."

CLOUDBERRIES

Cloudberries grow in the high, boggy meadows across the far north.

They make fruits with between five and twenty-five "bobbles".

The ripe fruits are a golden yellow colour. They are tasty eaten fresh or made into jam.

All the way back, Wulf kept stopping to pick even more berries.

Close to the Troll Bridge, Vik heard Flek barking up ahead. Peering over a rock, he saw two huge monsters guarding the bridge. Flek bravely yapped and nipped their feet.

"T-T-Trolls!" Freya squeaked for the second time that day.

Vik smiled as he watched Flek snapping at the ugly Trolls.

"I'm not so sure!" he said. "Do exactly what I tell you and we'll be all right..."

Five minutes later, Freya stepped into the early evening sunshine and walked calmly towards the bridge.

The enormous Trolls barred her way and began to chant:

"WE'LL BISH YOU AND BOSH YOU AND BASH YOU AND BEAT YOU, AND WHEN WE'VE FINISHED, WE'RE GOING TO EAT YOU!"

"Oh! You don't want to eat ickle me!" Freya told the Trolls in her sweetest girly voice. "If you wait a minute my brother will be along. He's *much* bigger than me and *much* more tasty."

The Trolls hadn't expected this!

"Here's something to keep you going." Freya tossed a few fruits in the air and ran – trit-trot, trit-trot – across the bridge to the safety of the other side.

As the Trolls picked up the fruits and ate them, Vik stepped out into the sunshine.

The Trolls leapt in
front of him and sang:

"WE'LL BISH YOU AND BOSH
YOU AND BASH YOU AND
BEAT YOU, AND WHEN
WE'VE FINISHED, WE'RE
GOING TO EAT YOU!"

"Oh! You don't want to eat little me!" Vik told the Trolls in his nicest, politest voice. "If you wait a minute my brother will be along. He's *much* bigger than me and *much* more tasty."

The Trolls scratched their huge, hairy heads.

"Here's something to keep you going." Vik scattered a few fruits on the ground, then he and Flek ran — trit-trot, trit-trot — across the bridge to the safety of the other side.

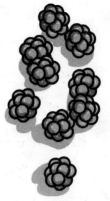

The Trolls picked up the fruits and ate them, until Wulf came bumbling round the corner into the sunshine.

"A-ha!" roared the Trolls, taking up their positions and howling their chant:

"WE'LL BISH YOU AND BOSH YOU AND BASH YOU AND BEAT YOU, AND WHEN WE'VE FINISHED, WE'RE GOING TO EAT YOU!"

Wulf puffed himself up and faced the monsters. "I'm not scared of Trolls!" he roared, as he charged towards them. It was enough to frighten the great god Thor himself!

39

Vik and Freya giggled as they watched from behind a juniper bush.

Wulf barged into the Trolls and knocked them over on the dusty path.

As the fight raged, the Trolls' leafy costumes came apart and fell over the side of the bridge into the deep ravine below.

"It's Barny and Sig, those two horrible boys from Ormsvik!" said Freya, surprised.

Vik smiled. "I knew they weren't Trolls, but they'll still give Wulf a good fight!"

"You left me to fight Barny and Sig on my own," Wulf grumbled as he came – trit-trot, trit-trot – over the bridge. He was covered in sticky blobs of cloudberry.

Wulf held out his empty backpack. "I've lost all my berries!"

"They're in your hair!" laughed Freya.

Vik slapped Wulf on the back. "We knew you could handle those two ruffians," he said. "Here, have some of our berries."

They shared out all the berries until they each had the same amount.

"You haven't picked many," Mum said, looking in their baskets. "But they are very big and – mmmm! – very sweet."

"*I* found them!" Wulf chirped.

Mum gave the dusty, sticky,
black-eyed boy a great big hug.
"Well done! I'll have to tell your father
how clever and helpful you've been."

Vik could hardly
believe it. Wulf was the
one who had caused
all the trouble!

"*I* knew where to look for the best ones," Wulf boasted. He just had to let Mum know how clever he was! "You know? Over the bridge and up where the sun shines?"

"Oh," said Mum sweetly. "Do you mean the Troll Bridge?"

"Yes!" Wulf answered cheerfully, before he realised his mistake...

46

Mum picked up the broom and chased Wulf out of the house.

"I told you not to go over the Troll Bridge!" she yelled. "And did you listen? Wait till I tell your father about this..."

Vik smiled and popped a cloudberry into his mouth.

SHOO RAYNER

All priced at £3.99

The Viking Vik stories are available from all good bookshops,
or can be ordered direct from the publisher:
Orchard Books, PO BOX 29, Douglas IM99 1BQ
Credit card orders please telephone 01624 836000
or fax 01624 837033 or visit our internet site: www.orchardbooks.co.uk
or e-mail: bookshop@enterprise.net for details.

To order please quote title, author and ISBN
and your full name and address.
Cheques and postal orders should be made payable to 'Bookpost plc.'
Postage and packing is FREE within the UK
(overseas customers should add £2.00 per book).

Prices and availability are subject to change.